This Topsy and Tim book belongs to

_____

This title was previously published as part of the *Topsy and Tim Learnabout* series
Published by Ladybird Books Ltd
80 Strand London WC2R ORL
A Penguin Company

1 3 5 7 9 10 8 6 4 2

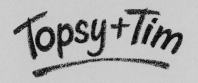

Meet the
Police

Jean and Gareth Adamson

One morning Topsy and Tim were
in a great hurry to get to school.
"The police are coming to talk to
us today," they told Mummy.

When they reached school a police
car was already there.
A policeman and a policewoman
got out.
"Can anyone tell us where to find
Miss Terry?" they asked.
"Why? What's she done?" said
Andy Anderson.

Topsy and Tim knew
where to find Miss Terry.
"Miss Terry is our teacher,"
they said.

"Police Constable Webb and Police Constable May have come to tell us all about the work that the police do," said Miss Terry.

"Do any of you children know the jobs that the police do?"

"They catch burglars," said
Andy Anderson.
"They look after traffic," said Tim.
"They find you when you are lost,"
said Topsy.
"Yes, we do all those things," said
PC Webb, "and we look after lost
things as well as lost children."

"Suppose Tim was walking down the street," said PC Webb, "and he found a purse full of money on the ground. What should he do?"

"Spend it?" said Andy Anderson.

"No," said PC Webb. "That would be very wrong. He should take it to a police station."

"Suppose Topsy was the one who
had lost the purse," said PC May.
"What should she do?"
None of the children knew.
"She should go to the police station
and tell them she had lost her purse,"
said PC May. "Then the police would
be able to give it back to her."

PC May asked Topsy and Tim
to help her pin up some pictures
of the police at work.
One of the pictures showed a
police dog.
"Have you got a police dog?"
asked Topsy.

"No," said PC May. "Police dogs belong to police dog handlers. The dogs are trained to find things that are lost or hidden. They are very clever."

PC Webb told the children that one of the most important jobs the police do is to come into schools and talk to children about safety.
"Some places are dangerous to play in," he said.

The children helped PC Webb think of some dangerous places.
"Don't play near deep water – you might fall in," said Kerry.
"Don't play by a railway line – a train might hit you," said little Stevie Dunton.
"Don't play on a building site – you could cut yourself on something sharp and rusty," said Louise Lewis.

"Always stay where your mother can keep an eye on you," said PC Webb, "and never ever talk to strangers. If a stranger tries to talk to you in the street or anywhere else, don't let them come near you."

"What is a stranger?" asked Tim.

"A stranger is someone you don't know," said PC Webb. "Most people are good and kind, but there are some people who like to take children away and hurt them.
So NEVER get into a stranger's car – even if they know your name and seem nice and friendly."

"If a stranger has tried to talk to you,
or asked you to get in his car, tell your
mummy or your teacher and they
should tell the police," said PC Webb.

PC May helped the children act a
play called Stranger-Danger.
Andy Anderson was a bad stranger.
"Will you help me find my lost puppy?"
he said to Vinda.
"No!" shouted Vinda, keeping out of
his way.

Rai was Vinda's daddy.
He took Vinda to the police
station to see PC Topsy
and PC Tim.
"My little girl says a stranger
frightened her," said Rai.
"Thank you for telling us,"
said Tim.
"We will try and catch that
bad man."

After the play it was time for
PC Webb and PC May to go back
to their police station.
The children waved goodbye.

On their way home from school that day Topsy saw something shiny on the pavement. It was a very pretty brooch. "Someone will be sad to have lost such a nice brooch," said Mummy.

"We must take it to the police station,"
said Tim. "Then the police can give it
back to the person who lost it."

"Hello," said the desk sergeant in the police station. "Can I help you?"
"Topsy's found a pretty brooch," said Tim. The desk sergeant took the brooch and wrote about it in her book.

She wrote down Topsy and Tim's address too.
"We will let you know if we find the owner," she said.

They went home and were having
tea when the phone rang.
Dad answered it.
It was the police to say that
they had found the owner
of the lost brooch.
"I wonder who it belonged to?"
said Mummy.

That night, when Topsy and Tim
were getting ready for bed, there
was a knock at the door. It was
Mrs Higley-Pigley.
"Thank you, Topsy and Tim,"
she said, "for finding my very special
brooch and for taking it to the police."